nd ready for trouble **BROUHAHA:** a noisy uproar **CACOPHO**

ng **CHAOS:** total confusion **DEFENESTRATION:** being topp

ED: unhappy, grumpy **DRENCHED:** dripping wet **FREEFALL:**

HORNSWOGGLED: tricked or deceived **HULLABALOO:**

wild mess and confusion **PEEVED:** annoyed **SCUFFLE:** a brie

HENANIGANS: mischievous tricks **SKEDADDLE:** run away,

own, all over the place **TRANQUIL:** quiet and peaceful **TRIC**

ACOPHONY: loud, clashing noises **CATERWAULING:** shrill

N: being toppled out a window **DEMOLISHED:** broken down,

FREEFALL: a drop through the air **HIGGLEDY-PIGGLED**

BALOO: a loud, wild uproar **KERFUFFLE**

FFLE: a brief struggle or fight **SER**

EDADDLE: run away, fast! **S**

rankish and ready for trouble

ATERWAULING: shrill screeching and yowling **CHAOS:** tot

PETEY and PRU and the HULLABALOO

by Ammi-Joan Paquette ✳ Illustrated by Joy Ang

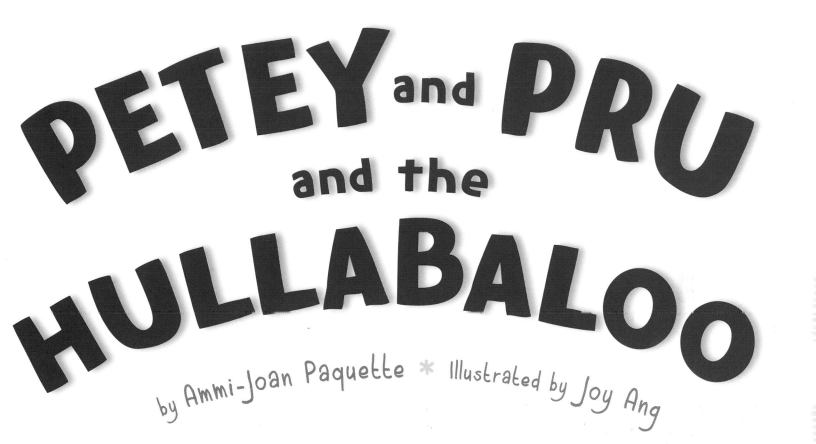

Clarion Books | Houghton Mifflin Harcourt | Boston New York

Clarion Books | 215 Park Avenue South, New York, New York 10003

Text copyright © 2013 by Ammi-Joan Paquette | Illustrations copyright © 2013 by Joy Ang

All rights reserved. | For information about permission to reproduce selections from this book,

write to Permissions, Houghton Mifflin Harcourt Publishing Company, 215 Park Avenue South, New York, New York 10003.

Clarion Books is an imprint of Houghton Mifflin Harcourt Publishing Company.

www.hmhbooks.com

The illustrations in this book were executed digitally. | The text was set in Aint Nothing Fancy.

Library of Congress Cataloging-in-Publication Data

Paquette, Ammi-Joan.

Petey and Pru and the hullabaloo / by Ammi-Joan Paquette; illustrated by Joy Ang.

p. cm.

Summary: In this celebration of sesquipedalian words, a quiet afternoon

erupts in a scuffle, which becomes a kerfuffle, which leads to a

hullabaloo for a dog, several cats, and two children.

ISBN 978-0-544-03888-2 (hardcover)

[1. Dogs—Fiction. 2. Cats—Fiction. 3. Vocabulary.]

I. Ang, Joy, illustrator. II. Title.

PZ7.P2119Pe 2013

[E]—dc23   2012038874

Manufactured in China

SCP 10 9 8 7 6 5 4 3 2 1

4500421293

To the Neve family
—A.-J.P.

To Jim & Ruth Stiksma
—J.A.

Petey is enjoying a **tranquil** afternoon:
peace and quiet and some light gardening.

Pru is feeling

tricksy.

She has a sneaky little plan.

Petey is
peeved.

There's only one thing to do.

The dog and cats are all
topsy-turvy.

Petey and Pru are all
higgledy-piggledy.

It's a
BROUHAHA!

Pru is delighted.

Perhaps a little more **mayhem** would add to the fun?

But that was one gush too much.

All the creatures
skedaddle.

Who is left?

One **drenched** Pru.

One **disgruntled** Petey.

And . . . one **demolished** garden.

Petey is crushed.

Petey has been

hornswoggled.

Petey has had enough!

23

They start with a **scuffle,**

which becomes a **kerfuffle,**

which leads to a **HULLABALOO!**

DEFENESTRATION!

Freefall . . .

Petey and Pru are safe.

How silly to waste all that effort on
SHENANIGANS!
Life is too short not to cherish true friendship.

All is well.

Petey is feeling **tranquil.** Perfectly content.

But . . .

Pru is feeling

TRICKSY!

BROUHAHA: a noisy uproar **CACOPHONY:** loud, clashing n

confusion **DEFENESTRATION:** being toppled out a window

grumpy **DRENCHED:** dripping wet **FREEFALL:** a drop throug

ricked or deceived **HULLABALOO:** a loud, wild uproar **KERF**

PEEVED: annoyed **SCUFFLE:** a brief struggle or fight **SERE**

ous tricks **SKEDADDLE:** run away, fast! **SWASH:** a great

TRANQUIL: quiet and peaceful **TRICKSY:** prankish and re

lashing noises **CATERWAULING:** shrill screeching and yowli

window **DEMOLISHED:** broken down, ruined **DISGRUNTL**

through the air **HIGGLEDY-PIGGLEDY:** jumbled, mixed up

ild uproar **KERFUFFLE:** a disturbance or fuss **MAYHEM:**

ight **SERENDIPITY:** an unexpected lucky happening **SHENAI**

r **TOPSY-TURVY:** upside down, all over the place **TRANQU**

BROUHAHA: a noisy uproar **CACOPHONY:** loud, clashing n

onfusion **DEFENESTRATION:** being toppled out a window

DRENCHED: dripping wet **FREEFALL:** a drop through the a

deceiv **HULLABALOO:** a loud, wild uproar **KERFUFFLE:**

SCUFF struggle or fight **SERENDIPITY:** an unexp

SWAS splash of water **TOPSY-TURVY:** upside d

rankish and ready for trouble **BROUHAHA:** a noisy uproar **C**

creeching and yowling **CHAOS:** total confusion **DEFENESTR**